A NOTE TO PARENTS

When your children are ready to "step into reading," giving them the right books—and lots of them—is as crucial as giving them the right food to eat. **Step into Reading Books** present exciting stories and information reinforced with lively, colorful illustrations that make learning to read fun, satisfying, and worthwhile. They are priced so that acquiring an entire library of them is affordable. And they are beginning readers with an important difference—they're written on four levels.

Step 1 Books, with their very large type and extremely simple vocabulary, have been created for the very youngest readers. **Step 2 Books** are both longer and slightly more difficult. **Step 3 Books,** written to mid-second-grade reading levels, are for the child who has acquired even greater reading skills. **Step 4 Books** offer exciting nonfiction for the increasingly proficient reader.

Children develop at different ages. **Step into Reading Books,** with their four levels of reading, are designed to help children become good—and interested—readers *faster*. The grade levels assigned to the four steps—preschool through grade 1 for Step 1, grades 1 through 3 for Step 2, grades 2 and 3 for Step 3, and grades 2 through 4 for Step 4—are intended only as guides. Some children move through all four steps very rapidly; others climb the steps over a period of several years. These books will help your child "step into reading" in style!

To "Mr. Dud,"
our own ebony sentinel
—*S. M.*

For Forrest Lange
—*C. R. B.*

Text copyright © 1989 by Clyde Robert Bulla. Illustrations copyright © 1989 by Susan Magurn. All rights reserved under International and Pan-American Copyright Conventions. Published in the United States by Random House, Inc., New York, and simultaneously in Canada by Random House of Canada Limited, Toronto.

Library of Congress Cataloging-in-Publication Data:
Bulla, Clyde Robert. Singing Sam/by Clyde Robert Bulla ; illustrated by Susan Magurn. p. cm.— (Step into reading. A Step 3 book) SUMMARY: Tired of caring for his new dog, a spoiled boy gives him to a young girl who discovers that the dog can sing. ISBN: 0-394-81977-2 (pbk.); 0-394-91977-7 (lib. bdg.) [1. Dogs—Fiction. 2. Behavior—Fiction.] I. Magurn, Susan, ill. II. Title. III. Series: Step into reading. Step 3 book. PZ7.B912Si 1989 [E]—dc19 88-19758

Manufactured in the United States of America   1 2 3 4 5 6 7 8 9 0

STEP INTO READING is a trademark of Random House, Inc.

Step into Reading

Singing Sam

by Clyde Robert Bulla
illustrated by Susan Magurn

A Step 3 Book

Random House 🏠 New York

Rob had a room full of toys. His father
and mother had given them to him.

But Rob was tired of his toys.

One of his friends had a turtle. "I want
one too," said Rob.

His father and mother gave him a
turtle.

For a while Rob liked his turtle. Then
he began to grow tired of it.

"You can't do much with a turtle," he said. "Remember the little ducks we saw in the pet shop? What I really want is a duck."

His father and mother gave the turtle away to the boy next door. They gave Rob a little duck.

For a while he liked his duck. Then he began to grow tired of it.

"You can't do much with a duck," he said. "What I really want is a dog."

His father and mother gave the duck to a girl down the street. They gave Rob a dog.

The dog was a black-and-white puppy with big brown eyes and floppy ears. His name was Sam.

"I like him—I like him!" said Rob. "A dog is the best pet of all."

For a while they had good times together. Then Rob began to grow tired of his puppy.

"You don't take care of him," said Rob's mother. "You forget to feed him, and you don't fill his water dish."

"You don't play with him anymore," said his father.

"I'm too busy," said Rob. "I have to go to school. I have to see my friends."

While Rob was busy, Sam was alone in the backyard. No one came to play with him or pet him or talk to him.

One day he found the gate open. He ran away.

Before long he was lost. He came to a yard in front of a little house. He was hot and tired, and he lay down on the grass.

A girl came out of the house. Sam went to her.

She sat down. He put his head on her knee. She stroked his floppy ears.

A woman came to the door.

"Look, Mother," said the girl. "Isn't he beautiful?"

"Yes," said the woman. "Whose dog is he, Amy?"

The girl looked at the tag on the dog's neck. She read, "'My name is Sam. I live at 487 Oak Street.'"

"Oak Street is a long walk from here,"
said her mother.

"Poor Sam," said Amy. "You must be
tired."

She fed him and gave him water.

"Now we must take him home," said
her mother.

"I wish he could stay," said Amy.

"So do I," said her mother, "but he is
not ours."

They got into the car. Amy rode in the
back and held Sam on her lap.

They stopped at 487 Oak Street.

Rob and his father and mother came
out of the house.

"Is this your dog?" asked Amy.

"Yes, it is," said Rob.

She opened the door. Sam got out.
But he did not run to Rob. He looked
back at Amy.

"Where did you find him?" asked Rob's father.

"At First Avenue and Green Street," said Amy. "That is where I live."

Rob looked at Sam. "You ran away," he said. "Bad dog. Maybe I don't want you back."

"Don't you want him?" asked Amy.

"I don't know if I do or not," said Rob.

"If you don't want him," said Amy, "I know someone who does."

"Amy," said her mother, "we have to go."

"Good-bye, Sam," said Amy.

They drove away.

"I didn't want to leave Sam," said Amy. "I don't think that boy is good to him."

When they got home, she was sad. She picked up a book, but she didn't want to read. She looked at the piano, but she didn't want to play.

She went out and sat on the porch.

A man drove up. There was a boy in the car. There was a dog in the car too.

It was Rob, his father, and Sam!

Sam jumped out of the car. Amy ran and picked him up.

Amy's mother came out.

Rob's father said, "My boy doesn't want a dog now. What he really wants is a pony. So I thought—"

"Yes?" said Amy.

"So if you'd like to have Sam," said Rob's father, "I'll leave him with you."

"You *will*?" said Amy.

"Yes," said Rob's father.

"Mother," said Amy, "is it all right?"

"It's all right," said her mother.

"Oh, thank you!" said Amy. "Thank you, thank you!"

Amy and Sam were happy together.
Every day they went for a walk.

Every day she combed him and
brushed him.

When she came home from school, he was there to meet her.

When she did her homework, he lay at her feet.

She told her mother, "Sam likes everything I like. He even likes music."

"How do you know?" asked her mother.

"He listens when I play the piano," said Amy.

Her teacher had given her a new piece to play. It was "The Happy Farmer."

She played it for Sam. He listened. He sat up and closed his eyes. And then—he began to sing!

It was not howling or barking. It was not very loud. He put his head back and went, *"Oo-oo-oo!"*

"Mother!" cried Amy. "Come and listen!"

"He can almost sing a tune," said Amy's mother.

Amy's grandfather came to see them.

"I have a surprise for you," said Amy.

She played her new piece. Sam sat up
and began to sing.

"Remarkable!" said Grandfather.
"This is really remarkable!"

He said to Amy's mother, "I know a
man who has a television show. I'm going
to tell him about this."

The television man called himself
Uncle Fred. His show was *Uncle Fred
and His Animal Friends.* He came to
hear Sam.

Amy played the piano, and Sam sang.

"This dog is good," said Uncle Fred.
"I want him on my show."

So Sam and Amy went on television.
She played "The Happy Farmer," and
he sang.

There were other animals on the show.
There was a dancing chicken.

There was a cat that walked a wire.

There was a pig that jumped rope.
But Sam won first prize. He won a big cup
and some money, too.

Thousands of people saw him on
the show.

And one of them was Rob.

"Look!" he said. "It's Sam!"

"And there is the girl who brought
him home," said his mother.

"I didn't know he could sing," said Rob.

He called his friends on the telephone. "Did you see Singing Sam on Uncle Fred's show? That's my dog."

The next day he and his father went to
Amy's house. She and Sam were playing
in the yard.

"Hello, Sam," said Rob. "Hello, old
boy."

"We saw him on television," said
Rob's father. "He was very good, Amy,
and so were you."

"Thank you," said Amy. "We think he
is going to be a star. Uncle Fred wants
him on the next show."

"But he isn't your dog," said Rob. "He
was mine all the time."

"He is not yours," said Amy.

"Let's talk about this," said Rob's father.
Amy called her mother.

"Rob says Sam is *his* dog," she said.

"My boy did say he wanted to give
Sam away," said Rob's father, "but that
isn't what he meant."

"No," said Rob. "It isn't what I meant."

"He was disappointed when Sam ran away," said Rob's father. "He wanted to punish him."

"Yes," said Rob, "but I don't want to punish him now."

"So he wants his dog back," said Rob's father.

"You can't have him!" said Amy.

"Amy," said her mother, "if the boy has changed his mind, you don't want to keep his dog, do you?"

"But it isn't fair!" said Amy.

Her mother asked Rob's father, "Do *you* think it's fair?"

"I'm trying to be fair to my boy," said Rob's father.

Rob pulled Sam away from Amy and put him into the car. Rob's father got in, and they drove away.

That night Rob gave a party. All his friends were there.

"I want you to meet Singing Sam," he said. "Maybe you saw him on television. Sam is my dog. Do you want to hear him sing?"

"Yes!" said his friends.

"All right, Sam," said Rob. "Sing."

But Sam didn't sing. He tried to hide in a corner.

"How do I get him to sing?" asked Rob.

"I don't know," said his father.

"I don't know," said his mother.

Uncle Fred came to Rob's house. "I hear Sam is your dog now," he said. "I want him on my next show."

"He won't sing," said Rob.

"Bring him down to the television station," said Uncle Fred. "We'll see what we can do."

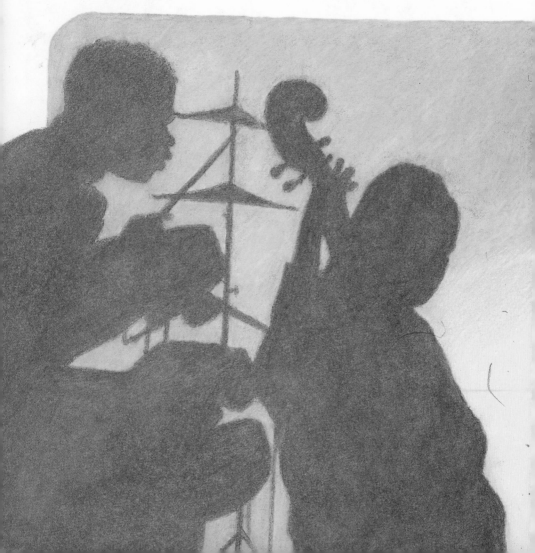

They took him to the station.
"He needs music," said Uncle Fred.
A band played.
"Sing, Sam," said Rob.
Sam hid under a chair.

"That is too much music," said Uncle Fred.

A woman played the piano.

"Sing, Sam," said Rob.

But Sam didn't sing.

"Come on, boy," said Uncle Fred.
"Come on, Sam."

At last he said, "I give up. I don't think this dog will ever sing again."

Rob and his father and mother took Sam out to the car.

"Bad dog!" said Rob.

"What shall we do with him?" asked Rob's mother.

"I don't care," said Rob.

"The girl wanted him," said his father. "Shall we take him back to her?"

Rob said again, "I don't care."

They went to Amy's house.

Amy came to the door.

"Sam!" she cried. Then she stopped.

"Would you like to have him?" asked
Rob's father.

"Why?" asked Amy. "So you can take
him away again?"

"I don't want him," said Rob.

"You might change your mind," she said.

"No," he said. "What I really want is
a pony."

"Then Sam is mine?" she asked.

"Yes," he said.

"Let me hear you say it," she said.

"All right," said Rob. "Sam is your
dog. But he won't be on television
anymore because he can't sing."

He and his father and mother
went away.

Amy hugged Sam.

"Did you hear what they said?" she
asked her mother. "They can't take him
away again, can they?"

"No," said her mother. "Now Sam really belongs to you."

"Good Sam," said Amy. "You're mine now. It doesn't matter to me whether you can sing or not."

Amy held Sam on her lap.

She combed and brushed him.

She played "The Happy Farmer" for
him on the piano. And all at once he sat up.
He closed his eyes. He began to go,
"*Oo-oo-oo!*"

"Listen!" said Amy.

"Sam is singing!" said her mother.

"I think he sings when he is happy,"
said Amy. "You *are* happy, Sam, aren't
you?"

And Sam barked and wagged his tail.

DATE DUE

JE 08 '92	NO 21 '95	DE 7 '99	
MY 21 '92	AP 02 '96	JAN 18	
AG 13 '92	AG 10 '96	FE 15 '00	
SE 21 '92	OC 21 '97	FE 17 '00	
OC 21 '92	DE 2 '97	SE 26 '00	
OC 28 '92	JA 28 '98	NOV 02 '00	
DE 09 '92	MY 20 '98	FE 06 '01	
MY 08 '93	SE 15 '98	MR 07 '02	
JY 09 '93	JA 26 '99	JE 13 '02	
AG 17 '93	MR 4 '99		
FE 18 '94	MR 31 '99		
SE 01 '94	MY 18 '99		
OC 29 '94	JE 18 '99		
NO 22 '94	AG 23 '99		
AP 11 '95	OC 21 '99		
JE 21 '95	NO 18 '99		
NO 07 '95			